IN

A TEDDY BEAR'S PICNIC

and other stories

GEOFFREY HAYES

PATRICK

IN

A TEDDY BEAR'S PICNIC

and other stories

A TOON BOOK BY

GEOFFREY HAYES

TOON BOOKS IS AN IMPRINT OF CANDLEWICK PRESS

For Will-yum,
finally, a bear book just for you.

Editorial Director: FRANÇOISE MOULY

Book Design: FRANÇOISE MOULY & JONATHAN BENNETT

GEOFFREY HAYES' artwork was drawn in colored pencil.

Library of Congress Cataloging-in-Publication Data:
Hayes, Geoffrey.
Patrick in A teddy bear's picnic and other stories : a Toon Book / by Geoffrey Hayes.
p. cm.
Summary: The further adventures of Patrick the little teddy bear as he goes on a picnic with his mother, tries to avoid his nap, goes to the bakery to buy cookies, and contends with the bullying Big Bear.
ISBN 978-1-935179-09-2 (alk. paper)
1. Graphic novels. [1. Graphic novels. 2. Teddy bears–Fiction. 3. Mother and child–Fiction. 4. Bullies–Fiction.] I. Title. II. Title: Teddy bear's picnic and other stories.
PZ7.7.H39Pit 2011
[E]–dc22
2010040209
ISBN 13: 978-1-935179-09-2 ISBN 10: 1-935179-09-8
11 12 13 14 15 16 TWP 10 9 8 7 6 5 4 3 2

www.TOON-BOOKS.com

PATRICK
IN
A TEDDY BEAR'S PICNIC
Bye, Patrick. Take care of Mama for me.
I will.

Is he coming back?
Yes, of course he is.
But now I've got you all to myself!
STOP, Ma! Hee, hee, hee!
How about a picnic?
I'll go get my stuff!
Let's go!

Let's just bring *one* toy in the picnic basket.
My ***scooter***!
Very ***funny***, Patrick!
I know! The little boat Daddy made!

SLOW DOWN!
WAIT! Did you put ***cookies*** in the basket?

I sure *did*.
And bread and cheese.
What *else*?
Apples and iced tea.
What *else*?
I can't tell you. It's a *surprise*!
ROAR!
PATRICK!

The park is for birds, too.
I don't want them pooping on my head!
This is a good spot.

I can see Grandma's house.

No, you can't. Grandma lives in Piedmont.
No, I can. Really.

Can we eat the cookies *first*?
First, look in the basket.
BALLOONS!
A *RED* one and a *BLUE* one!
FWEEEEE
You do it!
MA! Look how the wind makes it *wobble*!

OOOF!!
Come back!
BIG BEAR!
May I have my balloon... *please*!
NO!
I want to hear it go...
POP!

MA!!
Big Bear popped my balloon!
That big bully! Well, we have another one.

But I want the red one!
It's my favorite color!
Come, now. You'll feel better after you eat.
SNIFF!

I love all these little flowers.
Me too.

I'll pick some for you!
Pretty!
MA!
A **bug** flew on my paw.
Oh! A lady bug. Isn't she **pretty**?
OOPS! She flew away!

Here.
I'm going to play with my **boat**!
Sail, little boat.
Not ***that*** far!
KONK!

Ma, the water is too **fast** for my boat.
Let's play hide-and-go-seek.
I'll hide and you can be "*it*."
Okay. But don't go far.
Count to 20.
No...to 10.
No...to **15**!
Ready or not ...
here I Come!

No Patrick under the picnic blanket...
No Patrick behind the tree...
Give up?
WOOOOSH!
!
Nuts!

Slow down!
These puddles make good SPLASHES!
SPLASH!
And the rain is not cold!
SPLASH!
Look at you!
SPLASH!
SPLASH!

You're taking those wet clothes off *right here*!
WHEEE!!
I'm *naked*!
LA, LA, LA!
Oops!
What am I going to do with you?

Ma, I did not sail my boat very much!
Well, a picnic doesn't have to be in the park.
Do you know the best thing about a picnic in the house?
Nothing can get away.
Not even you!
STOP, Ma! Hee, hee, hee!
THE END

PATRICK
But I was in the middle of ***playing***!
You'll feel better after a rest.
Ma, can I come out ***now***?
Yes, if you feel rested.

HAS A NAP

THE END

PATRICK
AND BIG BEAR
ROAR!
Today I am a *dragon*!
ROAR!
Patrick, will you go to the store for me?
ROAR!

Way down *there*?
It's not far. We need cookies for lunch.
Here is a dollar.
What if I run into *Big Bear*?

But you're a *dragon*. Let's hear that dragon roar!

ROAR!
Ooow!

ROAR!
Hey, Stripey-Pants!
Give me that dollar!
Please, Big Bear. I'm going to buy cookies for Ma.
Are *not*!
Am *so*!

That's **MY** dollar!
It is *not*!

WHAM!

OLLIE'S
OPEN
CANDY, COOKIES & COMIC BOOKS
PHEW!

Good day, Patrick. What can I do for you?
Ma sent me to buy **cookies**.
Sure, what kind?
One of those...one of those...
...and **that** one with the little red things on top.
What is it?
Big Bear is after me.
He is, is he?

Well, you can scoot out the **back** door.
Tell your Ma hello for me.
I will.
There you are, Stripey-Pants!
You **owe** me that bag of cookies!
I do **NOT**!
OOPS!

I know you are *here*, Stripey-Pants.
I'll find you!
And *then* you'll be sorry!
LOOK! A cookie with little red things on top!
Yum!
But you're a *DRAGON*!

ROAR!!
I don't owe **YOU** ***anything***! You owe **ME** a cookie!
What a ***pig***!

Daddy, do you want to hear my ***dragon roar***?
ROAR!
Ooow!
So, did you run into Big Bear?
No! He ran into ***ME***!
THE END

ABOUT THE AUTHOR

GEOFFREY HAYES has written and illustrated more than forty children's books, including the extremely popular series of early readers *Otto and Uncle Tooth*, the classic *Bear by Himself*, and *When the Wind Blew* by Caldecott Medal-winning author Margaret Wise Brown. His Benny and Penny titles for TOON Books are bestsellers and have garnered multiple awards. In 2010, *Benny and Penny in The Big No-No*! received the prestigious Theodor Seuss Geisel Award, given to "the most distinguished book for beginning readers published during the preceding year."

One of Geoffrey's happiest childhood memories is going on morning picnics with his mother and brother to the local park.

PATRICK HAS ANOTHER NAP
But I took a nap yesterday!
Can't I skip it today, Ma? Can't I?
But I'm not even a tiny bit sleepy!
Nuts!
This doesn't make any sense.
THE END

TIPS FOR PARENTS AND TEACHERS:

HOW TO READ COMICS WITH KIDS

Kids *love* comics! They are naturally drawn to the details in the pictures, which make them want to read the words. Comics beg for repeated readings and let both emerging and reluctant readers enjoy complex stories with a rich vocabulary. But since comics have their own grammar, here are a few tips for reading them with kids:

GUIDE YOUNG READERS: Use your finger to show your place in the text, but keep it at the bottom of the speaking character so it doesn't hide the very important facial expressions.

HAM IT UP! Think of the comic book story as a play and don't hesitate to read with expression and intonation. Assign parts or get kids to supply the sound effects, a great way to reinforce phonics skills.

LET THEM GUESS. Comics provide lots of context for the words, so emerging readers can make informed guesses. Like jigsaw puzzles, comics ask readers to make connections, so check a young audience's understanding by asking "What's this character thinking?" (but don't be surprised if a kid finds some of the comics' subtle details faster than you).

TALK ABOUT THE PICTURES. Point out how the artist paces the story with pauses (silent panels) or speeded-up action (a burst of short panels). Discuss how the size and shape of the panels carry meaning.

ABOVE ALL, ENJOY! There is of course never one right way to read, so go for the shared pleasure. Once children make the story happen in their imagination, they have discovered the thrill of reading, and you won't be able to stop them. At that point, just go get them more books, and more comics.